WHAT READERS ARE SAYING ABOUT CHOOSE YOUR OWN ADVENTURE®!

"Choose Your Own Adventure is the best thing that has come along since books themselves."
—Alysha Beyer, age 11

"I didn't read much before, but now I read my Choose Your Own Adventure books almost every night."
—Chris Brogan, age 13

"I love the control I have over what happens next."
—Kosta Efstathiou, age 17

"Choose Your Own Adventure books are so much fun to read and collect—I want them all!"
—Brendan Davin, age 11

And teachers like this series, too:
"We have read and reread, worn thin, loved, loaned, bought for others, and donated to school libraries our Choose Your Own Adventure books."

**CHOOSE YOUR OWN ADVENTURE®—
AND MAKE READING MORE FUN!**

Bantam Books in the Choose Your Own Adventure® Series
Ask your bookseller for the books you have missed.

HURRICANE!

BY RICHARD BRIGHTFIELD

ILLUSTRATED BY LESLIE MORRILL

An Edward Packard Book

BANTAM BOOKS
TORONTO • NEW YORK • LONDON • SYDNEY • AUCKLAND

RL 5, IL age 12 and up

HURRICANE!

A Bantam Book / August 1988

CHOOSE YOUR OWN ADVENTURE® is a registered trademark of
Bantam Books, a division of Bantam Doubleday Dell Publishing Group, Inc.
Registered in U.S. Patent and Trademark
Office and elsewhere.

Original conception of Edward Packard.
Cover art by Catherine Huerta.
Inside illustrations by Leslie Morrill.

ISBN 0-553-27356-6

Published simultaneously in the United States and Canada

Bantam Books are published by Bantam Books, a division of Bantam Doubleday Dell Publishing Group, Inc. Its trademark, consisting of the
words "Bantam Books" and the portrayal of a rooster, is Registered in U.S.
Patent and Trademark Office and in other countries. Marca Registrada.
Bantam Books, 666 Fifth Avenue, New York, New York 10103.

PRINTED IN THE UNITED STATES OF AMERICA

O   0 9 8 7 6 5 4 3 2 1

For Jack Looney

Gulf of Mexico

CARIBBEAN

WARNING!!!

Do not read this book straight through from beginning to end! These pages contain many different adventures you may have when you try to locate a man who is missing at sea. From time to time as you read along you will be able to make choices. Your choices may lead to success or disaster.

The adventures you have will be the results of those choices. After you make your choice, follow the instructions to see what happens to you next.

Be careful! You set out to sea in the midst of hurricane warnings, and you may be swept up by the storm! Or, you may discover a time warp and a strange new world!

Good luck!

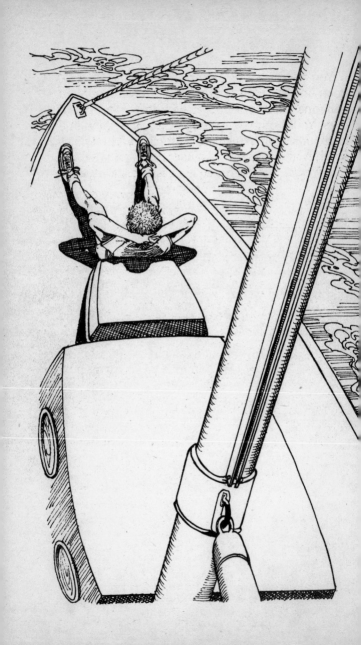

You are a treasure hunter. You search the Caribbean and the Gulf of Mexico for ancient, sunken galleons filled, you hope, with jewels and gold bars. Your home port is Key West, one island in a chain that stretches for more than a hundred miles south from the lower tip of Florida. Your boat, the *Sea Nettle,* on which you also live, is a thirty-foot sloop with an auxiliary engine.

There are reports of a hurricane approaching to the south, but there is no sign of it yet as you relax on the deck of your boat, watching a brilliant tropical sunset fade on the horizon.

As soon as it is completely dark, you go below deck to study some navigation charts in preparation for the next day's sail. You feel the boat sway slightly, but this movement is different from the way it rocks from an occasional small wave. Someone has come aboard unannounced!

You put down the map you are holding and head back up the ship's ladder to the deck. A girl about your own age is standing there.

"My name is Laura Sanford, and I . . . well . . . I need help!" she starts, a bit flustered.

"Come below," you say, "and tell me about it."

Turn to page 2.

2

Laura follows you below deck. "I've read about you in the newspapers," she begins, "about your searching for treasure and all that, I know it's an unusual request, but I was wondering if you'd be willing to help me. My father is missing . . . out in the Gulf."

"Have you gone to the Coast Guard?" you ask.

"I did," she replies. "They were polite and said they'd do everything they could. But right now I think they are more interested in getting out hurricane warnings."

"Has your father been missing long?" you ask.

"I lost radio contact with him a few days ago," she says.

"A few days? I'm sure he'll turn up soon," you say.

"You don't understand," she insists. "He knew he might be sailing into danger. He went out to investigate some mysterious signals. My father is a computer programmer. His hobby is amateur shortwave radio. A few months ago he started picking up what seemed to be a strange language in Morse code. He became fascinated—almost obsessed—with finding out what it was. The signals didn't seem to be in any language that he could figure out, even using his computer. It was more like an elaborate code of some sort. With a friend, another ham radio operator, my father managed to calculate approximately where the signals were coming from. A week ago he sailed out alone into the Gulf to investigate. Two days after he left, I lost radio contact with him."

Turn to page 6.

"I'll have to swim down and shake the anchor loose," you say.

"You mean you're going to dive down to the bottom?" Laura exclaims, a note of fear in her voice.

"Don't worry," you reassure her. "I'll hang on to the anchor line as I go down. It won't take me long, the water is not all that deep here."

You take out your scuba-diving equipment—air tank, mask, and weights—and lay them on the deck. Laura helps you put them on.

When you are ready, you slip over the side and swim down toward the anchor. You are almost to it when something off to your right catches your attention. It's a huge dome rising from the sea bottom!

Turn to page 18.

"Conrad will be bringing us food later," says Mr. Sanford. "Right now, I suggest that we rest. We'll need all our energy when it comes time to break out of here."

You try to rest, but you're too nervous. Everything has happened so quickly.

After what you guess to be about an hour, there is a soft knock at the cell door and the small panel used to pass the food through opens.

"I haven't been able to get the key to the cell just yet," Conrad whispers. "It will take me a couple of hours more. But I brought along a fire ax and I can try breaking the cell door open now. It might make a lot of noise though, and if there are any guards nearby, it's all over. What do you want to do?"

"I can't think clearly," Mr. Sanford says to you. "You make the decision!"

If you wait until Conrad gets the key, turn to page 82.

If you tell him to try to break the door open, turn to page 25.

"I admire your courage in approaching my dome," the bearded man says. "Perhaps, unlike Mr. Sanford, you—well, no matter. You are welcome."

"Where am I?" you ask, trying to sound calm.

"Ah, a good question," the man answers. "You are inside a pressurized dome that was built in Japan for use as the headquarters of a large undersea fish farm. My men and I intercepted it as it was being towed on the surface to a location off the American Gulf coast. We disposed of the towing crew and placed it here on the sea bottom as the nerve center for my own operations."

"But what—" you start.

"What is my operation?" the man interrupts. "I have developed a way of steering hurricanes to any spot on the Gulf or East coast of the United States. I went to the American government and offered them my services, but they just laughed at me. They nicknamed me Dr. Hurricane in jest, a name that I have taken for my own. Now I'll show them. Unless they pay me fifty million dollars every year, I'll hurl hurricanes at all the major cities on the coast."

Turn to page 9.

"Do you know where your father was headed?" you ask Laura.

"I have a duplicate of the chart he took with him," Laura says, taking out a folded sheet of paper from her purse and handing it to you. You unfold it on your chart table.

It shows most of the Gulf of Mexico and the northern part of the Caribbean. The channel between the western tip of Cuba and Yucatán is circled and a line going east and west is drawn just north of there.

"My guess is that he was headed toward some point along this horizontal line," she says.

You take down a chart of your own from the rack over the table and compare it with Laura's.

"This is really interesting," you say. "The line marked on your chart is approximately where a Spanish galleon, the *Valencia,* was sunk by pirates in the sixteenth century. I've always wanted to look for it. Maybe we can combine one search with the other."

"When can we leave?" she asks.

"Meet me here tomorrow morning," you say. "We'll leave at dawn."

Turn to page 12.

"Okay, let's go!" Conrad says.

You and Mr. Stanford quickly follow him down the corridor and up the stairway to the upper level. There you have to run as fast as you can to keep up with Conrad as he weaves between the geometric structures. Suddenly he stops and gestures for you all to crouch down. Up ahead is the dock, where several of Dr. Hurricane's men are working on one of the minisubs.

"You two wait here while I go over to those men," Conrad whispers. "When I signal, come running!"

Conrad walks down to the edge of the inside pool. The three men recognize him and keep working. Suddenly, without warning, Conrad shoves one of them into the water, then whirls and hits the second in the side of the neck with a karate chop. That one falls to the ground unconscious. The third man manages to dive out of the way and at the same time draw his gun. Conrad catches him with a kick to the side of the head just as he fires. But Conrad is hit! He sinks to the ground with a bullet in his shoulder.

Turn to page 20.

"You can direct hurricanes?" you gasp. "How can you do that?"

"If you really want to know," chuckles Dr. Hurricane, "my subs patrol the edges of the storm and fire rockets into it that explode and seed the storm with special chemicals I've developed. I use my computers here in this dome to calculate exactly where these explosions must take place."

"And you radio the locations to the subs with a special code, I'll bet," you say.

"My! You *are* bright," Dr. Hurricane exclaims. "That settles it. You *must* join my organization. I can make you rich beyond your wildest dreams. But if you don't join, I may have to be somewhat harsh with you."

If you pretend to join, turn to page 81.

If you refuse outright, turn to page 34.

10

"What's wrong with the boat?" Laura asks, very concerned.

"I'm not sure," you say. "Maybe there's some strong magnetic interference in this area." You drop anchor and wait.

Darkness comes quickly—as it does in the tropics. You both sit there listening to the gentle slap of water against the hull.

"There's a hurricane coming, but you'd never know it here," you say.

"It's what they call the calm before the storm," Laura says with a laugh. Then, with a more serious sound to her voice, she adds, "I sure hope we find my father soon. The stories I've heard about hurricanes scare me."

Suddenly, out of nowhere, a bright light appears across the water, directly ahead.

"Look! That must be another boat," Laura says. "It seems to be coming toward us awfully fast!"

"Too fast!" you exclaim. "It's about to crash into us!"

Turn to page 16.

You are awake at the first light of dawn, getting the *Sea Nettle* ready. Then, just as the sun's red arc appears above the eastern edge of the sea, you see Laura at the end of the pier coming rapidly toward you.

"I hope I haven't kept you waiting," she says when she arrives at the boat, slightly out of breath.

"No," you say. "I'm just about ready to cast off. We'll use the auxiliary and switch to sail once we get clear of the harbor."

Laura steps aboard and you start up the engine. Soon you are out beyond the reef, heading under sail toward the area in the Gulf indicated on her father's chart.

"According to your father's calculations, the signals could be coming from anywhere along the tip of Cuba to off the coast of Yucatán," you say. "We could start our search at either end. The coast of Yucatán is rocky and dangerous. On the other hand, the Cubans might not like our getting too close to their shore."

Laura shrugs. "I don't know," she says. "You decide."

If you head for the coast of Yucatán, turn to page 37.

If you head for the tip of Cuba, turn to page 22.

"Are you all right?" the man asks.

"I think so," you say, managing to push yourself up to a sitting position. "Except for my hands tied behind my back."

"I think we can do something about that," he says, getting up and coming over to you. "By the way, my name is Sanford. Lionel Sanford."

"Then you're Laura's father!"

Mr. Sanford looks at you with a shocked expression. "You know my daughter?" he asks.

"She came with me out here to look for you," you say. "In fact, she's somewhere above us, on the surface of the Gulf, in my boat."

"Then we have to get out of here and get to her!" he exclaims as he manages to get your hands free. "I've heard from the guards that Dr. Hurricane is about to steer the center of a hurricane past this exact spot, in preparation for directing it at one of the major cities on the coast."

"What can we do?" you ask.

"There's a spy in Dr. Hurricane's organization, a man named Conrad. He's going to help us escape—and soon!"

Turn to page 4.

The two figures drag you inside the minisub and tie you to the small deck behind the cockpit canopy. Then they pilot the sub through the arched entranceway into the dome.

The sub heads down a tubular passageway. Then it rises directly upward, surfacing in the center of a wide pool.

The sub moves to the edge of the pool and the two wet-suited figures pull you out and onto a dock. They tie your hands behind your back and push you toward the door of a cube-shaped structure. Inside is a brightly lit and richly decorated office.

A middle-aged bearded man is sitting behind a wide, marble-topped desk. He beckons you. "Come in! Come in!" he says.

Turn to page 5.

16

Suddenly the light sinks into the water only a hundred feet in front of you. You can follow its course deep below the surface as it passes down under your boat. The light continues in that direction until it disappears somewhere beneath the sea.

"What *was* that!" Laura exclaims.

"It must be some kind of submarine," you say, "but I've never heard of one that could move that fast."

You both sit there for a long time staring into the water, wondering if the strange light will come back again. Finally you fall asleep on deck.

Turn to page 26.

You decide to use the raft. All of you struggle back up to the heaving deck. The *Sea Nettle* plunges bow-on into the base of each wave and is then thrown violently upward—only to come crashing down seconds before plunging into the next. The salt spray whips across the deck, almost blinding you. Somehow you manage to get the raft inflated with a hand pump and you all climb in.

The next wave is a monster. Tons of green water crash down on the deck, splintering the cockpit and smashing open the hatch. What feels like a giant hand picks up the raft and lifts it away from the boat. The *Sea Nettle*, now half filled with water, wallows in a deep trough for a few seconds, then with the next wave sinks straight down into the sea.

For the next two hours, the four of you cling to the raft, hoping that the colossal waves won't flip it over. The raft goes up and down over the waves like a car on a roller coaster. A torrential rain pelts you, making it hard to breathe.

Finally, just when you've almost given up hope, the storm seems to die down a bit. Though the sea is still very choppy, it is definitely calmer.

Turn to page 28.

18

Leaving the anchor line behind, you swim toward the dome. As you do, you try to figure out its size—maybe fifty feet high and just as wide. When you get closer, you notice something else. The surface is translucent and through it you can make out vague rectangular shapes. You swim right up to the surface of the dome and press your mask right up against it. The shapes are clearer and look like small buildings.

So far, you don't see any openings or outside features. There may be some on the other side of the dome, you think. Whatever it is—a government project of some sort perhaps—it could be dangerous. Something is telling you to go back to your boat—fast! On the other hand, the dome *is* fascinating, and it wouldn't take you long to swim around to the other side.

If you go back to free the anchor, turn to page 75.

If you swim around to the other side of the dome, turn to page 31.

You and Mr. Sanford dash over to help the wounded Conrad.

"Get me into the sub," he says, groaning with pain. "Another sub is due from the outside, and we have only a few minutes while the outer door to the dome is open."

You and Mr. Sanford carry him through the hatch of the sub. He slumps into the pilot's seat. You sit beside him in the copilot's seat. Mr. Sanford takes the jump seat behind you.

"I can't move my arm to operate this thing," Conrad says weakly. "You'll have to do it. The red lever is for direct underwater ascent and descent. The joystick works the same as an airplane's— push forward to go down and pull back to go up. Push it left to go left and . . . and. . ."

Conrad slumps forward, unconscious.

Mr. Sanford reaches over from behind and feels his pulse. "I was a medic in the navy and I have some experience with these things," he says. "His pulse is strong. He's lost some blood, but I think he'll be all right."

"We'll all be all right if we can get out of here," you say. "Fortunately these controls seem simple enough."

Go on to the next page.

You push the red lever all the way forward. The sub instantly sinks below the water, going down fast. In a few seconds you are lined up with the tunnel leading to the outside. With the regular controls, you guide the sub forward, and in a few more seconds, you are at maximum speed.

You see the door to the outside up ahead—and it's still open!

But just when you think you are away free, you suddenly see another sub entering the tunnel from the outside. Your sub is speeding toward a head-on collision in the narrow tunnel!

Turn to page 36.

You check your compass readings and set a course for the western tip of Cuba.

"Do you think you can find this signal that your father was getting on my shortwave radio?" you ask.

"I'll try," Laura says. "The frequency is written down on the bottom of his chart."

You handle the boat while Laura goes below and works with the radio. After several minutes, her head pops up out of the hatch.

"I think I have it," she says.

You tie down the tiller and go below. You've listened to a lot of dots and dashes, but this signal is really strange.

"It's certainly not ordinary Morse code," you say. "But with some luck, we may discover what it really is."

You go back up topside and run up full sail. You sail all day, and late in the afternoon you are near your destination. With a major storm coming, the sea is strangely calm. The wind dies and you find yourselves drifting. You try to start up the engine, but your batteries are dead. And none of your navigational instruments are working!

Turn to page 10.

You are about to congratulate yourselves when a warning light flashes on the control panel. The ship is out of fuel!

Your sub bobs helplessly in the mounting seas. The waves seem to rush in and batter it from all sides. You wonder how long the sub can continue to stand up under the pounding of a major hurricane.

The End

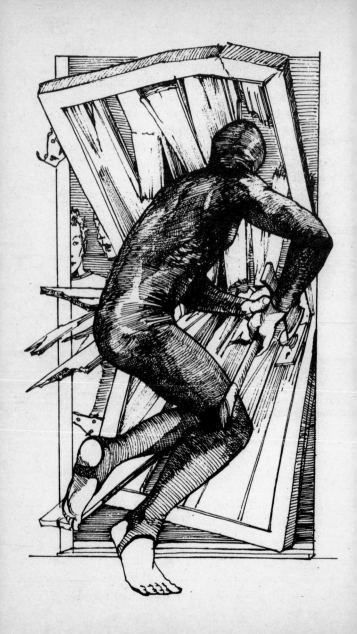

You tell Conrad to try to break down the door. "With the hurricane coming, I think we'd better take a chance and try it now," you say.

"All right then, stand back from the door!" Conrad says, lifting the ax over his head.

He brings the ax down full force against the door, right next to the lock. The noise of the blow reverberates through the narrow corridor outside the cell. Then silence. All three of you listen to hear if anyone is coming. Still silence.

"I think the door gave a little," Conrad says. "I'm going to give it a shove."

There is a dull thud as Conrad hits the door with his shoulder, followed by a splintering sound as the lock breaks and the door swings open.

Turn to page 8.

26

The glow of the early morning sun wakes you up the next day. The sea is much rougher and there is a stiff breeze blowing from the northeast. You check the barometer and see that it's falling dramatically—a sure sign of an approaching hurricane.

Laura is also awake and she sees the worried look on your face.

"What's the matter?" she asks, her voice quivering a bit.

"I think we're in for a big blow," you say.

"What are we going to do?" she asks.

"I think we'd better pull up anchor and head back to Key West," you answer.

But when you try to pull up the anchor, it won't come up.

"The anchor's stuck on something. This should make it come loose," you say, jerking the line back and forth.

But it doesn't budge!

Turn to page 3.

The sudden ascent leaves you breathless. But there's no time to rest. You see the *Sea Nettle* bobbing on the choppy sea not far away.

Conrad groans and opens his eyes.

"Where are we?" he asks.

"We're on the surface of the Gulf," you say. "There's my boat over there."

"Is my daughter all alone on your boat?" asks Mr. Sanford.

"She is," you answer. "I'm heading for it now."

"The fuel gauge looks pretty low," Conrad says. "In fact, we're almost empty."

"We got out here, anyway," you say, trying to remain hopeful.

Suddenly a big wave slams broadside into the small sub, knocking it all the way over on its side before it rights itself.

"The sea is getting rough," says Mr. Sanford. "I hope Laura is all right."

"We'd better hurry. We're a sitting duck if Dr. Hurricane's other subs show up," Conrad says. "If we can get the girl aboard this sub, we can try to make a run for it."

"Or we could all transfer to my boat and abandon the sub altogether," you say. "I think the *Sea Nettle* might be able to ride out the storm."

If you decide to pick up Laura and make a run for it in the sub, turn to page 41.

If you decide to transfer to the Sea Nettle *and abandon the sub, turn to page 58.*

"Is the worst part over?" Laura gasps, gazing out at the storm.

"I wish it were," answers her father. "I think we're just going into the 'eye' of the hurricane. We're going to have to go through the whole thing again!"

"I don't understand," Laura says.

"Hurricanes are like gigantic rotating donuts, hundreds of miles across. They go counterclockwise in the Northern Hemisphere and clockwise in the Southern Hemisphere," Mr. Sanford explains. "The hole or 'eye' at the center is usually about twenty-five miles wide. But the sea is calmer there, though still very choppy. Winds of around eighty miles per hour are in the outer ring."

"At least if we're in the eye, we'll get a short rest," you add.

Half an hour later, a bit of hazy sunlight streaks down from above. Hundreds of birds are flying around or floating in the water. Some even try to land on the raft. Towering gray walls of dark clouds surround you on all sides.

"The hurricane is too high for the birds to fly over, so they try to follow the eye until the storm peters out," you explain.

"It's too bad we can't do the same thing," Laura says.

"We might if we could keep this raft going at thirty miles an hour," you say.

Suddenly there is a strange sound in the air.

"Look!" Laura shouts, "A plane!"

Turn to page 35.

You decide to stay with the boat. You fasten down the hatch cover as tightly as you can. Then everyone finds a spot in the cabin where they can hold on while the *Sea Nettle* is tossed violently about in the angry sea.

Suddenly a huge wave crashes down on the deck, busting open the hatch and pouring a heavy stream of water into the cabin. Instantly you are all up to your waists in the swirling water. You struggle to get up the ladder to the deck, but another wave beats you back down.

You try again. This time you get to the deck just in time to see a gigantic wave loom up in front of you. The *Sea Nettle* is swept almost straight up into the air. It hangs suspended there for a moment at the top of the wave—and then plummets down into the deep trough on the other side. The bow cuts into the water and keeps going—straight into the depths of the sea.

The End

Laura rushes, wide-eyed, up the ladder to the deck.

"Something smashed through the wall of the cabin!" she screams.

You start down the ladder and stop. The lantern below has gone out, but you can hear the sound of water rushing into the cabin.

"We must have hit a reef or some offshore rocks!" you say as you climb back up to the deck.

"Are we going to drown?" Laura exclaims.

"Not if I can get this raft inflated," you say, pulling it out of its storage locker on deck and working on it with a hand pump.

You get the raft inflated just as the deck of the *Sea Nettle* sinks to the level of the surface of the Gulf. You and Laura have no trouble getting into the raft just as your boat slips under the waves for good.

"At least we're not too far from the coast," you say. "I could see it faintly up ahead before sunset."

You and Laura paddle steadily toward the coast. The water is choppy, but the currents seem to be in your favor. After a while, you see a point of light ahead. As far as you can tell, it's on the shore—if it were on a boat, it would be bobbing up and down. You paddle toward it. Soon you hear the surf ahead and can see the dim outline of the cliffs behind a pale strip of beach.

All at once a wave catches your raft and lifts it high up into the air.

Turn to page 38.

You follow the curve of the dome around to the other side. There you see a high, arched entrance to the dome. As you float, suspended, trying to figure out what to do, you feel a rush of water as something—or things—speed by, just over your head. They are miniature submarines of some sort.

Then one of them arcs around and comes back. As it does, two figures in wet suits and scuba gear come out of the sub. They swim directly toward you. You realize, too late, that there's no chance of escape.

Turn to page 15.

"Pirates!" Laura exclaims under her breath.

That's exactly what the figures look like—old-fashioned pirates, with long hair and beards and ragged tunics, and leggings. They don't smell too good either—a mixture of unwashed clothes and liquor.

"What'll we do?" Laura whispers.

"Hark there and be still, young 'uns!" barks the tallest of the three pirates. "We be takin' ye back aboard the *Python* ere we sail."

"What is he saying?" Laura whispers.

"I think they are going to take us prisoner," you whisper back. "Maybe we should make a run for it."

"If we do, they might kill us," Laura whispers. "Do you see those sabers they have? But maybe they're just pretending to be pirates. After all, this is the twentieth century."

If you make a run for it, turn to page 48.

If you go with them, turn to page 71.

34

You refuse to join Dr. Hurricane. "There's no way that I'm going to help you with your schemes!" you exclaim.

"That's too bad," says Dr. Hurricane with an evil laugh. "You'll have some time—in fact, a long time—to regret that decision." He presses a button on the side of his desk and several of his men come rushing into the room.

"Take our visitor to the guest chamber," he orders with another laugh.

The men grab you roughly and push you back out the door. Your hands are still tied behind your back. They lead you away from the cube-shaped structure and through a number of narrow passageways between other geometric structures. These could be where Dr. Hurricane stores his rockets and chemicals, you think.

Finally you come to an opening in the floor with a stairway going down. They push you down it, going single file until you reach a corridor at the bottom. At the end of the corridor is a cell. They open the door and shove you inside so hard that you stumble, breaking the fall with your shoulder as you go down. The door is slammed shut behind you.

You lie there stunned for a few minutes. Then, as your eyes get used to the dim light, you see that there's a man crouched in the corner.

Turn to page 13.

A large navy seaplane buzzes by not far over your head. It banks around and comes back, its nose into the wind. The force of the wind holds it almost stationary above the raft. A sailor with an amplified megaphone leans out of an open cargo door in the side of the plane.

"We can't land. The water's too rough," he shouts. "Stand by to grab hold of the air-sea rescue net."

Moments later, the bottom of a broad net at the end of a heavy rope comes tumbling down into the water. The plane maneuvers so that the net sweeps over the raft. You all grab hold and hang on for dear life.

The net rises slowly, and many hands grab hold to pull all of you in when you are close enough to the door.

"Lucky we spotted you," says one of the several navy technicians inside. "We fly in and out of the eye of each hurricane to gather data and get fixes on their exact centers. We send the information via satellite to the National Hurricane Center in Miami."

Turn to page 89.

You must avoid the other sub. But how? You can't keep going straight, that's for sure! You have a split second to decide whether to go up or down. If you pull back too sharply, you may crash into the ceiling of the tunnel. Or, even worse, the other sub may try to do the same thing and the two of you will collide.

You can also dive and hope that the other ship will go up.

If you pull back sharply and try to go over the other sub, turn to page 68.

If you dive down to the bottom of the tunnel, turn to page 50.

You decide to head for Yucatán. You sail all day and by evening you are off the coast of Mexico. You can just barely see the cliffs of the Yucatán headlands way in the distance.

"We'll anchor here for the night," you say.

The sun drops below the horizon, leaving long plumes of crimson in its wake. Darkness comes quickly after that. Laura bunks down in the cabin below while you doze on the deck, watching the full moon rise on the horizon.

Suddenly there is a crash, and the *Sea Nettle* is jolted from one end to the other!

Turn to page 30.

You and Laura lie flat on the raft and hold on as it rides the top of a wave toward the shore like a surfboard. Moments later you are tossed free of the raft and find yourselves standing waist-deep in the surf—struggling to keep from being carried back out by the strong undertow. You are knocked down by the next wave breaking on the shore but manage to crawl up onto the beach.

You both lie there for a while, catching your breath and listening to the surf booming not far away. Then you both struggle to your feet. Up above you, at the edge of a high cliff, is the dark shape of a pyramid, spectacularly silhouetted by a bright orange tropical moon rising behind it.

At the base of the pyramid is a point of light, probably the one you saw from the sea. In the bright moonlight, you find a trail from the beach going up through the rocks toward the pyramid.

Soon you are at the top of the cliff, near the pyramid. Now you see that the light at the base is definitely a doorway.

"What should we do?" Laura asks.

"I'm not sure," you answer. "We could climb to the top of the pyramid and get a good look around. We could probably see for miles from there. Or we could investigate what's inside that door."

Laura looks at you expectantly and waits for your decision.

If you climb to the top of the pyramid, turn to page 88.

If you enter the pyramid, turn to page 66.

You make sure that no one else is coming, then you and Laura continue down the tunnel. At the end is a brightly lit entranceway. Inside you find some kind of control room. On the wall opposite, an observation window looks down on a wide chamber filled with machinery and scientific equipment. Next to the window is a stairway going down to the floor level of the wide chamber.

"This looks more like a power station than anything else," you say. "I wonder what it's doing inside of what looks like an ancient Mayan pyramid."

"If this really *is* an ancient pyramid," Laura says.

"It certainly looks like one on the outside," you say. "We could go down and see if we can find out what this machinery is actually doing."

"Or," Laura says hopefully, "we could get out of here altogether!"

If you go down and examine the machinery, turn to page 45.

If you go back outside, turn to page 52.

You decide to pick up Laura and make a run for it in the sub.

Carefully you maneuver the sub in the swelling sea to a position beside the *Sea Nettle* and take Laura aboard. She is barely inside when two of Dr. Hurricane's other subs appear on the surface. You go full throttle forward—toward Key West—as the other subs come after you.

The other subs start to close in on you. Without warning, Conrad jams his fist on the control panel and your sub veers sharply to the left. Less than a second later a small but deadly missile streaks by, missing you by inches.

"That was close," Conrad says. "But two can play that game. Take over the controls for a while."

Conrad makes his way somewhat painfully to the back of the sub. A few seconds later, your ship shudders for a moment as Conrad fires the sub's rear missile. The pursuing sub closest to you tries to dodge, but the missile hits it head-on. The sub disintegrates in a huge explosion. The other sub turns in an arc and heads in the other direction.

Turn to page 23.

"You went back in time when you fell into that machine," says Professor Ashley. "We are now in the tenth century, if my calculations are correct—just before the super hurricane that, I believe, destroyed the great Mayan civilization. I created the time warp to come back here—now—and see for myself what actually happened. Unfortunately a few other things have slipped through the warp."

"Like some Sioux Indians?" you say.

"And some others, pirates and such, I'm afraid," says the professor. "But *this* is the period I've been aiming for."

"But Professor," Laura says. "Even if you see that your theory about the hurricane is correct, will anyone believe that you really came back in time?"

Go on to the next page.

"I see what you mean," says the professor, now deep in thought. "Anyway, back to the business at hand. The priest with the torch thinks we are gods come to save the Mayans from Harakan. We'll have to do something about that—the Indians might attack us if they find out that we're not. And another thing, the top of this pyramid may not be the best place to be when the full force of the hurricane strikes. Unfortunately there isn't a 'window' back into the space-time continuum for another seventy-two minutes. The storm should hit before then. If we go down to the plaza and over to the Indian village, we may not be able to get back up here where the focus of the warp is located. My! I really don't know what to do," he says to you.

If you stay on top of the pyramid,
turn to page 69.

If you go down to the Indian village,
turn to page 78.

You decide to go down and have a look at the machinery. With Laura right behind you, you start down the narrow stairway to the floor below. The hum of the machinery is much louder now. At the bottom of the stairway, the machines tower over you. You look down the narrow passageways between them. At the end of one such passageway, a bright purple light seems to be rising and falling. You and Laura start down toward it. You don't get far.

Suddenly a panel drops open in the side of the machine right in front of you. An invisible force grabs hold of you and starts to drag you toward it. You both grab a metal bar on the side of the machine right next to you. The force seems to get stronger and stronger—Laura is pulled loose. You grab for her and lose your own grip. Both of you go flying into the machine. The last thing you see is someone running down the corridor behind you. He is hollering, "Watch out!"

But he's too late.

Turn to page 63.

Torrents of stinging water wash over the deck as the *Sea Nettle* heels over on its side. You grab hold of a cleat to keep from being washed overboard. Bits of wood go flying past your head as the mast snaps in two and most of the rigging is blown away. Fortunately the others are below when the wave hits. They are tossed around in the cabin, but no one is hurt.

When the boat rights itself, you manage to crawl below and break out the sea anchor, a device that looks like a small parachute at the end of a rope. Back up on deck, you tie down one end of the sea anchor and toss the rest overboard. With the sea anchor trailing behind, the *Sea Nettle* slowly faces into the wind. Now at least the waves aren't hitting you broadside where they can do the most damage.

Conrad shouts something up to you from the hatch, but you can't hear him over the howling sea. You climb back down with the others, closing the hatch behind you.

Go on to the next page.

"I hate to say it, but I don't think this boat is going to hold together in this storm," Conrad says.

"What can we do?" Laura sobs.

"We can stay with the *Sea Nettle* and take our chances," you say. "Or we can get off in the life raft." It's possible that the raft may be better able to survive this kind of sea. But you must decide quickly. If you wait until the last minute, you may not be able to get off the *Sea Nettle* at all!

If you decide to stay with the Sea Nettle, *turn to page 29.*

If you go on the raft, turn to page 17.

48

You and Laura dash into the jungle. Almost at once, you find a narrow path and run along it. You can hear the shouts and curses of the pirates as they come after you. Soon you are both out of breath. You go sideways off the path and crouch there, listening. You can hear only the wind.

You rest for a short while, then you start again—going deeper into the jungle. Then you find your way blocked by a swampy area. You try to wade through, up to your waists in the murky water. Suddenly you start to sink into the soft, slimy mud on the bottom. It's like quicksand—no, worse than quicksand. At least in quicksand you can lie flat on your back and "float" while you gradually work your way out. This stuff is like a demonic force, steadily pulling you down into the deadly muck.

You struggle to free yourselves, but you just sink deeper and deeper until your heads are finally below the surface.

The End

You feel some strong force spinning you and suddenly you come flying out of the machine inside the professor's laboratory. You land on the floor and roll forward. Except for scrapes and bruises, you feel all right. You get to your feet just as Laura comes tumbling out followed by the professor, who miraculously lands on his feet. You guess that he's used to this sort of thing.

It takes you a few seconds to look around and see that the machines are red-hot—some shooting showers of sparks out of their tops.

"Maximum overload!" the professor hollers. "We've got to get out of here fast!"

Turn to page 57.

50

You push the control stick forward, and instantly the ship dives to the bottom of the tunnel. At the same moment, the other sub shoots upward. Even so, you miss each other by only inches and your sub scrapes bottom for a moment with a screeching sound. Seconds later you are through the outer door and free of the dome. You put your sub into an almost vertical climb at full speed.

The miniature sub breaks through the surface of the water like a missile shot from below. It shoots several feet into the air and splashes down again on the surface with a jolt.

Turn to page 27.

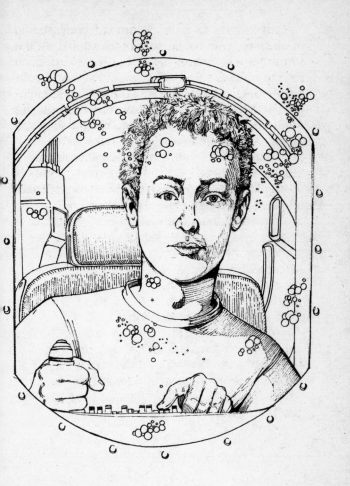

52

You decide to go back outside, and you and Laura leave the pyramid. A stiff wind is blowing from the ocean and clouds are racing across the moon.

"There's something a little too strange about this whole setup here," you say. "We'd better try to find some safe shelter for the night—especially with a hurricane brewing."

"If we head inland, maybe we'll find a road," Laura suggests.

"I think I see a path over there," you say. "We'll follow it into the jungle and see where it leads."

You start down the path. It branches in many places and you try to follow what looks like the most-traveled route—as best you can in the dark. After a while, though, you realize that you must be going around in circles. You try to find your way back to the pyramid, but you can't. Then you stumble into a wide clearing.

You are standing there, trying to figure out what to do, when several dark figures come out of the jungle on the other side and start toward you. For a few moments the moon comes from behind a cloud. Laura lets out a frightened gasp as it lights up the figures.

Turn to page 32.

The explosion blows you and Laura overboard. Miraculously, neither of you is hurt, and you both tread water near what remains of your boat, helplessly watching a thick billow of black smoke rise from its bow.

"The *Sea Nettle* is between us and the shore where the soldiers are," Laura says. "If we swim mostly underwater, we could make it to the other side of the bay."

"You're right," you say. "But I hate to just let the *Sea Nettle* burn."

If you follow Laura's advice and swim to the other shore, turn to page 108.

If you climb back aboard the Sea Nettle *and try to put out the fire, turn to page 101.*

"The way that Indian is coming up the side of the pyramid is scary," Laura says, standing by your side. "He looks like he's *gliding* up—and not even using his hands!"

A strong gust of wind blows across the face of the pyramid, sending showers of flaming sparks from the priest's torches into the air. Now he is almost to where you are standing, just below the top.

"GLI BAL TATUM TEPEU HARAKAN!" he shouts up at you.

"I wonder what he's saying," Laura says.

"I could have sworn he said hurricane," you say.

"He did," says a voice from the shadows inside the small temple behind you. "The word *hurricane* comes from the name of the Mayan storm god, Harakan."

You turn as a man steps half out of the doorway of the temple. It's the man who shouted a warning as you were pulled into the machine inside the pyramid.

"Who are you?" Laura asks.

"My name is Ashley, *Professor* Ashley, actually."

"Are *you* responsible for us being here?" Laura asks him accusingly.

"It's not my fault if you got caught in the time warp," he says in an indignant tone of voice.

"Time warp!" Laura exclaims. "Are you trying to tell me we've gone back in time?"

Turn to page 42.

56

The pirates scurry around the deck, hoisting up the sails. The ship begins to move almost at once, and in a matter of minutes you are heading through the inlet into the ocean.

As soon as you are out of the bay, the *Python* hits rough seas. You hold on tight to keep from being thrown by the pitching of the deck. But the ship sails on, and after a while you see the first pale fingers of a gray, cloudy dawn. Some of the topsails blow away in the wind, but the captain still insists on full sail. Soon it is light enough to see, and the ocean is a mass of foam in all directions.

"I don't understand how they expect to attack anybody in this storm," you say to Laura.

Suddenly you spot a distant sail across the raging waters.

"There she be!" bellows the captain.

Turn to page 61.

Just as you get out of the pyramid, a series of explosions knock you flat. The top of the pyramid is spouting a column of fire like a miniature volcano.

As if this weren't enough, the hurricane is now hitting full force. Trees are beginning to blow away and stones are flying through the air. It seems as bad as the hurricane that could have destroyed the Mayan civilization.

"I have another laboratory—the entrance is down among the rocks!" the professor shouts, getting back to his feet. "We'll be safe there!"

After the experience with the professor's time warp, you wonder if you can really trust him. On the other hand, the jungle is probably not the safest place to be in a hurricane.

If you follow the professor to his other laboratory, turn to page 94.

If you decide to take your chances in the jungle, turn to page 96.

You decide to transfer to the *Sea Nettle*. After all, the sub is almost out of fuel.

You manage to get close to your boat during a momentary lull in the storm. A little maneuvering and you are right alongside. You pop open the hatch, and you and Mr. Sanford help Conrad out of the sub and over the railing of the boat. You find Laura crouched below in a corner of the cabin, her face as white as a ghost's. But she is overjoyed to see her father and she soon recovers.

Meanwhile you go back and set the sub's controls on automatic, slam the hatch closed, and jump back to the deck of the *Sea Nettle*. The sub takes off at full speed across the mounting waves just as two of Dr. Hurricane's subs surface not far away.

Dr. Hurricane's men think that you are still in the sub and are trying to get away. The two subs chase the empty runaway, speeding side by side. They are almost to it when you see a large wave pick up one of the pursuing subs and crash it down on top of the other. There is a flash of light and a muffled explosion—for a second louder than the howling wind—as the two subs blow up and disintegrate.

At almost the same moment, your anchor line snaps and the *Sea Nettle* is itself caught broadside by a huge wave.

Turn to page 46.

Dr. Hurricane shoves Conrad into the cell and slams the door behind him.

"So all of you thought you were smart, did you?" Dr. Hurricane cackles. "Now you'll see how clever *I* am. The door to your cell is watertight. Are your feet getting a little wet?"

They *are* getting wet. Water is pouring into the cell through open pipes along the base of the wall. The cell is filling up!

"There's got to be some way we can stop it," you say, feeling the ends of the pipes under the water.

"Maybe we can put pieces of cloth into the ends of the pipes," Conrad says.

"It's worth a try," you say, pulling off your socks and trying to stuff them into the ends of the pipes. It works for a while, but the water pressure in the pipes is too strong.

Slowly but relentlessly the cell fills up with water.

Later, your lifeless body floats suspended in the water as a panel slides open in the side of the flooded cell and a huge shark noses its way in—eager to feed!

The End

A cheer goes up from all hands on deck. It takes two hours for the *Python* to catch up with the other ship, which is a large galleon, much larger than the pirate ship.

You see several flashes of light from the side of the galleon, and a second or so later you hear the booming sounds above the wind.

"They're shooting at us!" cries Laura.

Spouts of water from the cannon balls landing close to the *Python* are almost immediately lost in the waves. One shot slams into the side of the pirate ship right at the waterline. The pirate ship fires its own salvo, but their shots are way off.

Suddenly the pirate ship swings hard to starboard and plunges forward through the waves on a collision course with the galleon.

Turn to page 73.

62

You decide to stay aboard the pirate ship. As if to keep you from changing your mind, the two ships pull free of each other. You can hear the screams and shouts above you as the grappling lines snap, sending many of the pirates plunging into the sea. The pirates left on the *Python,* including the pirate captain, are struggling with what's left of the rigging.

Suddenly a hatchway in front of you opens and a woman's face peers out. She seems almost as surprised to see you and Laura as you are to see her.

"You must be the other prisoners I was hearing about," she says. "My name's Carla. I was captured from another ship. I have learned many things about these pirates and their ship. Right now we must get to the stern and see if we can get into the skiff—if it's still being towed behind the ship."

With Carla leading, you and Laura weave across the heaving deck to the back of the ship. The skiff is still there, though almost invisible in the spray.

"Our only chance is to slide down the towrope," Carla shouts over the roar of the storm. "I'll go first."

She slips over the aft railing and slides down the rope. You and Laura follow, going hand over hand above the hissing foam below.

Turn to page 79.

You and Laura are spinning through the machine in a tornadolike vortex. What is happening? you wonder. You spin faster and faster until you pass out from dizziness.

When you come to, you are lying on a hard surface. Laura is next to you—a shocked expression on her face. You are on top of a pyramid, as far as you can tell, the same pyramid you entered a short time ago. You get up and look around. A few steps in front of you is a very steep stairway that seems to go almost straight down. You turn and see a one-story temple behind you, built on top of the pyramid. You can't remember seeing the temple on the pyramid before. The front of the temple is covered with elaborate carvings, all painted bright and garish colors.

You look back over the front edge. Far below is a wide plaza filled with Indians, Mayan Indians this time, most of them carrying lighted torches. One of them, possibly a priest, to judge from what he is wearing, is rising up the steep stairway toward you, a flaming torch in his hands.

Turn to page 55.

You feel your body being pulled in all directions at once. Then whatever it is stops abruptly. You're surprised to find yourself still on the top of the pyramid.

Something large and luminous starts to materialize at the back of the platform. It has the outlines of some sort of building. At first you can see the moon right through the walls, then they become solid.

"What is it?" Laura gasps.

"It looks like a temple—a Mayan temple," you say.

The figures holding you and Laura also start to appear. They look like Mayan priests in elaborate costumes. One of them is holding a long obsidian knife.

An altar in the shape of a reclining jaguar forms at the top of the stairway—and the priests are pulling you and Laura toward it.

Turn to page 87.

66

You decide to enter the pyramid. Cautiously you peer through the entrance door. Inside is a long corridor, brightly lit at the other end. You can hear a strange, throbbing hum, like the operation of electrical machinery. Numerous deep niches have been cut in the sides of the corridor.

You and Laura step inside and carefully move toward the bright light. You are halfway there when the shapes of several figures loom up in front of you, momentarily blocking the light.

You both quickly duck into one of the side niches and crouch down. You watch from the shadows as a line of figures marches past.

"They look like Indians," Laura whispers.

"Yes, but the wrong kind of Indians for here," you whisper back. "On this coast they should be *Mayan* Indians. Those look like Plains Indians, probably Sioux, from the midwestern United States. No Mayan ever wore a feathered warbonnet like that."

The last Indian files past where you are hiding. You peek around the corner of the niche. They are just at the entrance to the tunnel to the outside—but instead of going outside, they seem to suddenly vanish at the end of the tunnel.

Go on to the next page.

"One second they were there, and the next second they're gone," you say as you turn to Laura, still crouched behind you. "It's as if they were some kind of hologram."

"You mean like a photographic illusion?" she asks.

"Yes. Or perhaps they just got caught in the wrong time and place by magic," you say, laughing. "Maybe we'll find our answer at the end of this tunnel."

Turn to page 40.

You pull the throttle back and the sub zooms up. Unfortunately the pilot of the other sub decides to do the same thing.

WHAM! Both subs collide and explode in one titanic blast.

The walls of the underwater tunnel are blown outward in all directions, smashing the underpart of the dome and setting fire to many of the rockets that Dr. Hurricane has stored there. Suddenly the whole dome erupts in a huge explosion that blows a column of water and steam hundreds of feet high on the surface of the sea.

You gave your life, but at least you put an end to Dr. Hurricane and his evil plans.

The End

You decide to stay on top of the pyramid. It seems like the best way to get back to your own time. You watch the priest, who is still standing on the stairway just below the top of the pyramid. His torch has blown out in the rising wind. Professor Ashley shouts some things at him in Mayan. The priest flings the burnt-out torch away and, this time using both his hands and his feet, scampers back down.

"What did you say?" Laura asks.

"I told him to tell his people that the gods are displeased and to flee deep into the jungle or they will all be destroyed."

"What about us?" Laura asks.

"There's a pit in the corner inside the temple," the professor says. "We'll duck in there until the storm blows over."

Turn to page 74.

"Spies!" Laura exclaims. "We're not—"

"Silence!" the woman commands. "I'll tell you when to speak. Now, what are you doing on this island?"

"We're trying to find shelter from the hurricane," you say.

"Yes, my colonel, the hurricane is coming," says one of the soldiers. "The men are worried and—"

"Will you *shut up!*" the woman hollers, standing up and banging her fist on the table. "Get down to the beach and help get the barges ready—before I have you shot!"

The soldier dashes toward the beach.

"Cowards!" the woman exclaims, sitting down again heavily. "We must stick to my timetable. The landing to liberate our country from its illegal and immoral government has been planned to the second. Hurricane or no hurricane, nothing must stop it."

"What country is that?" Laura asks.

"That's a military secret," the woman says. "Now, if both of you will join our invasion forces, we will not be forced to try you before a military court as spies. And remember, if you are convicted, you will be shot by a firing squad before we leave."

If you agree to join the invasion force, turn to page 106.

If you decide to take your chances with the military court, turn to page 90.

You decide to go with the pirates. Suddenly you realize that they could be another mirage. How long will they last, you wonder. Probably not long. The others vanished after a short while.

"Don't worry," you whisper to Laura. "I think I understand the—"

"Belay that talk and get movin'," one of the pirates orders, shoving you forward.

The pirates seem to have no trouble finding their way through the jungle, and soon you are back on the top of the cliff. Down below is a sheltered cove, and a pirate ship is at anchor in the center of it. Even at this distance, when the moon comes out for a few seconds, you can spot the Jolly Roger, with its skull and crossbones, flapping at the top of the mast.

The pirates lead you down a path through the rocks to the beach below. Then they push you into a skiff and row you across to the pirate ship, where they haul you up onto the deck. A tall, fully bearded man with chains of gold jewelry hanging across his bare chest and a brightly colored sash tied around his waist above his breeches is clearly the captain.

"Shall I haul 'em below and put 'em in irons, Cap'n?" asks one of the pirates, pointing at you.

"Don't bother with that!" the captain bellows. "Let's get under sail. Storm or no storm, we've got a meeting with a galleon filled with gold."

Turn to page 56.

A few seconds later, the bow of the *Python* smashes deep into the side of the galleon, then pulls partway out, leaving a gaping hole. The pirates toss their ropes with grappling hooks up over the railing of the galleon—several feet higher than that of the *Python*. The pirates swarm up the ropes and onto the deck of the larger ship. A couple of them dash past you and through the hole in its side. You realize that you have a split second to decide whether to follow them into the galleon or stay with the pirate ship.

If you go aboard the galleon, turn to page 95.

*If you stay aboard the pirate ship,
turn to page 62.*

You all rush inside to the corner of the temple and jump down into the pit carefully cut into the stone. The wind sounds as though an express train is roaring by on top of you. Pieces of stone fly off the facade of the temple, and the stone roof begins to sound like it's being ripped apart. A heavy slab of stone comes crashing down from the ceiling and falls on top of your hiding place, trapping you all inside the pit. More pieces of stone collapse on top of it.

Professor Ashley is elated. He seems totally oblivious to the danger you are in. "This proves my theory beyond a shadow of a doubt. When I get back—"

"If you get back," you interrupt. "If any of us gets back."

The noise and violence over your head reaches a peak. Suddenly all the stones covering you fly off—even the heavy slab—as all of you are blown up into the air.

Turn to page 49.

As fascinating as the dome is, you don't have time to explore it now with a hurricane coming. You return to the anchor line and continue to follow it down. The anchor turns out to be snagged on a large outcrop of coral. You work it loose and swim with it back up to the *Sea Nettle*.

You check the falling barometer and scan the ragged clouds racing by barely above the top of the mast.

"We don't have enough time to get back to Key West before the storm hits," you say, pulling out your charts. "Maybe we can find an island where we can lay over."

You locate one on your chart, then you run up full sail. The *Sea Nettle* skims over the water, running with the wind.

Then you see the island in the distance up ahead. You approach it on the lee side, the side protected from the full force of the wind. You struggle through a rough, confused sea and finally enter a wide, sheltered bay.

"This is perfect," you say. "We can—"

You are interrupted by loud booms from the shore. Several spouts erupt in the water around your boat. A line of men, all dressed in combat fatigues and all carrying rifles, runs out on the beach.

"What is this!" you exclaim in wonder. "Is there a war going on here?"

Suddenly the bow of the *Sea Nettle* takes a direct hit and explodes!

Turn to page 53.

76

Even above the screaming wind, you can hear the bullets whiz over your head and strike the tree behind you. Both you and Laura fall as if shot and lie still. You try to breathe as shallowly as possible, but your heart is beating like crazy.

"Attention!" a sharp command comes from behind the row of soldiers who have just fired the volley. "Assemble on the beach at once!"

All of the soldiers leave.

You and Laura lie there for a long time, not daring to move, as the sounds of the storm screech over your heads.

"Do you think they've all gone?" Laura says finally.

"I don't hear anything except the wind," you say.

Turn to page 91.

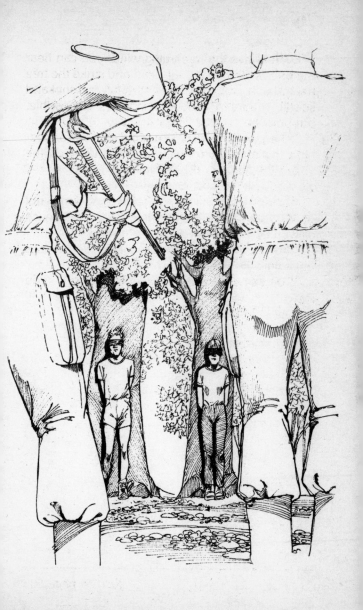

"I think we should go down to the Indian village," you say.

The three of you work your way down the steep side of the pyramid. The wind is doing its best to blow you off, but finally you reach the bottom.

"It looks as if all the natives have fled," you say.

"They're afraid of Harakan—not just the storm, but the fierce god himself," says the professor.

You all walk across the broad, smoothly paved plaza, now whipped by rain coming in gusty downpours. At the other side is the beginning of a wide, paved causeway raised above the undergrowth of the jungle. The causeway stretches straight as an arrow off into the distance. Following Professor Ashley, you and Laura start along it. The rain makes the surface slippery and, combined with the strong wind, makes it hard to stay on your feet. You go on for a long time. Finally, up ahead, you see the village.

Turn to page 84.

You are amazed at how quickly Laura swings along the towrope. She is no longer the frightened girl who started out on this trip. Perhaps Carla's example is giving her courage.

All of you make it to the bobbing skiff. Carla cuts the rope holding it to the pirate ship, and the skiff goes sailing away. And none too soon. Looking back, you see that the *Python* is listing far to one side. A wave catches it and the whole ship flips upside down in the sea. The upturned hull heaves up and down in the waves for a few seconds as if it were a surfacing whale, then sinks out of sight for good. The galleon has also disappeared into the storm.

The skiff, as small as it is, seems very seaworthy. It rides the waves well, and even when it starts to rain very heavily, you have no trouble bailing. You, Carla, and Laura take turns rowing and bailing.

"If we head in that direction, we'll reach an island," Carla says, pointing.

"How do you know?" Laura asks.

"I'm not really sure—call it intuition. Also, I was raised in these islands," Carla says.

You might as well take her word for it. Right now one direction seems as good as another. The main thing is to stay afloat.

Suddenly you are in the surf close to a beach. The skiff flips over, tossing all of you into the waves.

Turn to page 112.

Safe inside the cenote, the three of you sleep fitfully, huddled in the back of the cave, while the storm rages above. You try not to think of the unfortunate Mayans who were sacrificed here to the rain gods.

You are awakened the next morning by a shaft of bright sunlight streaming down into the cenote. You look up through the broad opening and see nothing but blue sky. The storm has passed.

You, Laura, and the professor go warily up to the surface and back to the village. It is a mess. The houses have all been uprooted and are either lying on their sides or are completely upside down. They are partially flattened, like huge baskets stepped on by giants. You don't see any Mayans. As far as you can tell, nearly the whole population has been wiped out.

You follow the causeway back to the pyramid and climb to the top. All that is left of the temple are a few large slabs of stone lying flat on the top platform. You wait all day, hoping to connect with the space-time continuum.

Turn to page 111.

"I'll join your organization," you tell Dr. Hurricane.

"Very good!" the doctor exclaims, rubbing his hands together in glee. "I have just the mission for you. Operational module X4K, one of my minisubs, is shorthanded. It is about to go out and seed the hurricane with iodide crystals."

Dr. Hurricane presses a button on the side of his desk, and almost at once two hulking creatures that would look at home in a horror movie appear at the door. You wonder how all three of you can fit into a minisub.

"Let me introduce Sam and Igor," Dr. Hurricane says. "They will show you the ropes."

Sam and Igor lead you out of the office and over to the dock, where several tiny subs are moored.

"We're going to take this one," Igor says. "The boxes of crystals are already loaded."

Turn to page 110.

You tell Conrad you'll wait for him to get the key.

"I'll be back in a couple of hours," Conrad whispers through the door. "I'm sure I can get it by then."

You and Mr. Sanford wait patiently. Then you hear footsteps in the hallway outside the cell. You hear the key in the lock and the cell door opens partway.

"It's Conrad," Mr. Sanford says. "But what—"

"You bet it's Conrad," an evil voice interrupts.

You'd recognize that voice anywhere—it's Dr. Hurricane!

Turn to page 60.

The village, like the plaza, is deserted. Most of the huts are already shaking in the strong winds.

"There's got to be a *cenote* nearby," says the professor. "If we can find it, we'll be safe."

"Cenote?" asks Laura.

"A cenote," says the professor, "is a natural well formed when the limestone crust collapses over an underground stream."

"You mean we're going to crawl down a well!" Laura exclaims.

"No. I mean . . . it's hard to explain," says the professor.

"There's a small path going off to the side there—between those two huts," you say, pointing.

"That must lead to the cenote," says Professor Ashley.

Turn to page 93.

You slam the door of the cockpit shut and, as fast as you can, start to shove the heavy boxes of crystals against it.

"Hey! What do you think you're doing!" Igor hollers through the door. You can hear them struggling to get it open, but it's wedged shut.

Luckily you find a tool kit fastened to the side wall. You take out a pair of heavy snippers.

"Go back to that boat you passed awhile ago, or I'm going to cut all the pipes and cables in here," you say.

Sam and Igor realize that the sub could become their tomb if you do. After a certain amount of cursing and swearing, they turn the sub around and head back.

Turn to page 105.

When the priests have you and Laura almost to the altar, you turn suddenly and do a quick back flip—a bit of jujitsu you learned a few years before. At the same time, you hold on to one of the priests and shove him up into the air with your legs. At the top of his arc, you let go, sending him flying over the altar. When he lands on the other side, he skids along the platform and over the edge. You can hear him hollering in Mayan as he slides all the way down the side of the pyramid.

The Indians holding Laura are so surprised that they relax their grip. She lets go with a hard kick to one of their ankles. You bounce back from your roll and give a karate chop to the side of the other's neck. The rest of the Indians stand there frozen in shock.

If you take this chance to try to get down the side of the pyramid, turn to page 97.

If you and Laura run inside the temple behind you, turn to page 99.

You and Laura climb to the top of the pyramid in the moonlight. It's a steep climb, and the sides are overgrown with moss and vines part of the way up.

When you get to the top, you find a wide platform. There is not much else there except a few scattered stones. The view, however, is spectacular. You can see way out over the ocean on one side and look across a seemingly endless jungle on the other. Low-flying clouds are blowing in at a great speed.

"This is definitely an ancient pyramid," you tell Laura as you turn to start back down.

Suddenly you are grabbed by an invisible force. Laura is, too. You struggle to pull away, but whatever it is, it's too strong!

Turn to page 64.

The plane flies high up over the towering walls of cloud that surround the eye and then down again to the naval station at Pensacola. Here the skies are still blue, with only some low-flying scud clouds blowing in—clouds that herald the approach of a hurricane. Conrad is rushed to the navy hospital for treatment of his shoulder.

"Thank you for helping us," Laura says to you. "I wish there were something we could do for you."

"Maybe when I get another boat—" you start.

"We'd love to go treasure hunting with you," they both say in unison.

The End

"So you won't join our forces! That proves that you *must* be spies. Take them to the drill field and have them shot!" the woman colonel shouts at the guards standing behind you.

"What about the trial you said we were going to get?" Laura asks.

"Trials? We don't need any stinking trials!" she shouts. "If I say you are guilty, you are guilty!"

The guards lead you away, their guns jabbing you in the back. When you are out of sight of the colonel, one of them whispers, "Don't worry, we'll fire over your heads. The madame colonel is a little upset over the coming storm. She doesn't like anyone or anything to interfere with her plans. But remember, when we fire, fall down as if you were shot—just in case any of her staff officers are watching."

The soldiers march you out of the palm trees and across a sandy field. They stand each of you against a tree and blindfold you.

Then, they stand back and open fire!

Turn to page 76.

The rain starts to come down in sheets as you both cautiously get up and pull off your blindfolds. The camp is completely deserted. The colonel's tent has been blown away by the wind.

Laura waits on land while you go down to the bay and swim out to the *Sea Nettle* through the choppy water and driving rain. You try to sail it to a cove at the end of the bay where it might have some protection from the storm. But the wind drives you ashore before you get there.

You jump clear and run back to where Laura is crouching in a deep ditch in a thick grove of palm trees. Maybe they will give you some protection, or maybe not. But it's the only place you can find to wait out the hurricane.

The End

You and Laura follow the professor down the path. You see a large circular opening in the ground up ahead. It must be, you think, two hundred feet across and more than fifty feet deep—with a pool at the bottom.

"Quick! There's an opening to a stairway cut in the stone over here," says the professor. "It must lead down to the bottom of the well."

You go down the long, underground stairway and come out on a shelf of rock a few feet above the water. A broad overhang of stone covers you above, with a shallow cave behind.

"We'll be out of the storm here," says the professor.

"Where are all the Mayans?" Laura asks. "You'd think this would be the first place they'd come in a severe storm."

"Ah yes, but they're afraid of the Chacs, the fierce gods of rain that live down here," says the professor. "And the ghosts of the many human sacrifices that they painted blue, weighted down with heavy gold jewelry, and hurled to their deaths in the pool from up above."

Turn to page 80.

You follow Professor Ashley down along the rocks to a round steel door set into the cliff. He presses a combination on the door lock and it swings inward. You all go through.

Inside is a smaller version of the laboratory inside the pyramid.

"This is my original laboratory. I worked here before I hollowed out the ancient pyramid," says the professor. "This whole chamber is a kind of time machine. I see from my instruments that the destruction of the pyramid has reversed the polarity of the local space-time continuum. That means that if I pull this lever . . ."

You see the fanatical gleam in his eyes, too late to stop him from pulling the lever.

Turn to page 107.

You and Laura scamper on hands and knees through the hole in the side of the galleon. The pirates that preceded you have disappeared, but you can hear the din and shouts of battle on the deck above you. There is a loud grinding and splintering sound behind you as the waves pull the pirate ship free of the galleon. The grappling lines snap, sending many of the pirates plunging into the sea. You hear the shouts and curses of the pirates left on the *Python* fade away as their ship is swept away from the galleon.

"The fighting seems to have died down up above," you say. "I wonder who's winning."

You look around. You are in a compartment filled with casks and crates. It is strangely quiet except for the sound of the sea. Suddenly two men dressed in light body armor and carrying rapiers appear at the door at the far end of the chamber. One of them says, "*Viene con nosotros, por favor:* Come with us, please."

Turn to page 103.

You and Laura head into the jungle looking for somewhere safe to wait out the storm.

You manage to find a good road cleared through the jungle. It definitely looks as though it must go somewhere. You and Laura start down it with the trees swaying wildly in the wind on both sides. An occasional burst of moonlight through the dark, rushing clouds illuminates the long stretch of road ahead.

You keep going as the storm gets worse. You begin to wonder why you haven't come to a town or a settlement. There must be one not far ahead, you think.

Now the sky has clouded over completely, and sheets of rain are starting to sweep by, lashing you and Laura in the face. Broken branches are strewn across the road, and here and there trees crash in the jungle.

Suddenly, above the sound of the wind, you hear fierce growls in front of you. You turn to retreat, but growls come from behind you also. A pack of jaguars has come out of the jungle—driven crazy by the storm. You see only their luminous eyes in the dark as they leap at you through the air.

The End

You and Laura scamper down the side of the pyramid. You are halfway down when you realize to your horror that there's a line of Mayan warriors climbing up after you from the bottom.

You look up and see the Mayan priests, knives in hand, coming down at you from the top.

In a desperate attempt to get away, you and Laura try crawling sideways along the side of the pyramid. You haven't gone far when your feet slip on the wet stone and you slide helplessly down, right into the razor-sharp, obsidian-tipped swords of the Mayans.

The End

It is early dawn of the next day when you and Laura finally step out of the structure. The storm has passed and the sunrise is spectacular in golds and yellows. You suddenly realize that Carla is missing. You search all around for her, but she is nowhere to be found.

"Do you think Carla was really a ghost or a spirit of some sort who came to rescue us?" Laura asks.

"I wonder if we'll ever find out," you say.

You do find that you are on an uninhabited island. The ground is covered with coconuts. At least you'll have enough to eat and drink until you are rescued.

The End

You grab Laura by the hand and pull her into the temple. Inside, flaming torches attached to the wall light up several large terra-cotta idols. You grab one and find that it's relatively light—probably hollow. You turn and smash it over the head of one of the Indians trying to run in the door— knocking him out. The rest of them draw back from the doorway. Laura helps you barricade it with the other idols.

A strong gust of wind hits the pyramid, blowing several of the Mayans off the edge of the platform. The others retreat, climbing down the stairway.

You and Laura wait for a few minutes. Then you cautiously crawl over the idols to the outside. There is no sign of the Mayans. The altar is gone and the temple itself is starting to fade.

What kind of strange illusion was that? you wonder.

Both of you hurry back down the pyramid and start off into the jungle.

Turn to page 96.

You and Laura swim back to the boat and climb aboard at the stern. You grab a bailing bucket, lean over the side to fill it with water, and run forward. Fortunately it's not as bad as you first thought. The bow has been partly blown away and several of the splintered timbers are smoldering. A few well-placed buckets of water and the fire is out. You just hope they don't lob another shell at you.

"Who are they!" Laura exclaims. "And why are they firing at us?"

Go on to the next page.

"I don't know," you say. "But we may find out soon. Look over there. A military patrol boat is coming toward us from the other end of the bay."

The boat pulls up alongside, and several soldiers dressed in camouflage uniforms jump aboard, guns in hand.

"All right, hands in the air!" one of them commands in a strange accent that you can't identify.

They take you and Laura aboard the patrol craft, which then heads toward the shore. When you get close enough, they make you jump into the water, waist deep, and wade ashore. Then they lead you through the palm trees to a large, khaki-colored campaign tent set up in a clearing.

In front of the tent, seated behind a small table covered with maps, is a woman dressed in a military uniform. Her jet black hair is tied back in a severe bun.

"Here are the spies we captured, my colonel," one of the soldiers says, saluting.

Turn to page 70.

The Spanish soldiers lead you up to the deck. It is bouncing up and down with the high waves. The few pirates left alive are surrendering, and the crew of the galleon is putting them in irons and taking them below. You are led to the stern of the ship and into an ornate cabin. An elaborately dressed gentleman greets you.

"Ah, come in, my friends. My name is Jose Garcia Maria Rodriguez de Silva. I am captain of this ship," he says, with a sweep of his hand. "As soon as some of my men saw you come aboard the *Valencia*, they knew you were prisoners of the pirates escaping their ship."

A sailor appears at the door of the cabin. He has a worried look on his face.

"You must excuse me for a moment," the captain says graciously. "I must talk with my first mate."

A discussion follows in Spanish between the captain and the mate. Then the captain turns back to you.

"My first mate says that the *Valencia* is breaking up in the heavy seas. Our cargo of gold is . . ."

Turn to page 114.

You force them to come alongside the *Sea Nettle,* where you pick up Laura. You toss out a few boxes of crystals to make room for her.

"Am I ever glad to see you!" she exclaims. "I'd given you up for dead, and I didn't know if I'd survive in this storm myself."

"Your father's alive, too," you say. "And I know we can rescue him."

Sam and Igor are forced to take you to the naval base at Key West. There they are arrested while you tell all the details about Dr. Hurricane's base.

The navy organizes a team of frogmen to rescue Laura's father, as well as put Dr. Hurricane out of business.

The End

You and Laura agree to join the invasion force, hoping to stall for time.

The soldiers lead you down to the beach where a row of open landing barges is lined up along the shore.

You join several soldiers on board one of the barges, and with a roar of motors, the whole line of steel barges moves out into the bay in single file. Yours is the first barge behind the colonel's command ship.

When your barge reaches the ocean, it starts getting tossed around like a cork on the foaming, confused seas. Several times it is almost swamped, but it still heads doggedly forward.

After a while, you can barely see the command ship, even though you know it's not far away. But you *can* see it when a huge wave bears down on it from the front.

The wave engulfs the command ship, which hangs there for a few moments on its side, then disappears beneath the surface. You watch in horror as the same wave bears down on you. Moments later, your barge is caught by the wave and tossed into the air. You and Laura are thrown free as it flips over and plunges belly down into the sea—sinking like a rock.

You both start swimming back toward the island, but you don't have a chance in the hurricane-driven waves.

The End

As the professor pulls the lever, you feel an electric shock go through your body. You are frozen to the spot where you are standing.

"What . . . have . . . you done?" you gasp.

The professor speaks with effort but also elation. "This time instead of going back to the past, we are going forward to the future—2000 years into the future."

"But I don't want to go to the future!" Laura shouts angrily.

"It's too late to stop it," Professor Ashley says.

"No, that can't be. . ." you say as you start to black out.

The End

You and Laura swim desperately for the other shore. You stay as much as you can underwater, only coming up for quick gulps of air when you have to.

The burning *Sea Nettle* drifts out of the way and the soldiers on the beach see you. They start firing in your direction. The second time you come up for air, you feel a sharp pain in your shoulder. You dive again. A bullet has made only a grazing flesh wound, but you are leaving a trail of blood in the water.

Suddenly you are being circled by several long, streamlined shapes—sharks! You swim as fast as you can. You've only got a short way to go to get to the shore.

You almost make it—but not quite.

The End

You follow Sam and Igor aboard the minisub. They have to squeeze between the boxes that fill the small cabin and through the narrow sliding door into the cockpit. You ride in the cabin with the crystals.

The sub dives immediately and goes through the tunnel to the outside. It zooms up to the surface and heads south. You catch a glimpse of the *Sea Nettle* bobbing in the waves off to the right— then it is left behind. You turn away from the porthole hoping Laura is all right.

"Break open one of the boxes!" Sam orders you through the open door to the cockpit. "Empty the crystals into the base of the rocket tube in the center of the cabin."

As you start to break open one of the boxes, you notice the rows of pipes and wires that are fastened to the low ceiling. Suddenly you get an idea!

Turn to page 85.

"I have a horrible feeling," says the professor, "that the connections between here and our own time have been broken. We've been gone a long time. If the space-time interrupter has overloaded, it might have blown up."

"Oh, no! You mean we could be stuck here for good!" Laura exclaims.

"In that case, I guess we'll just have to search for survivors and, if they let us, help them rebuild their society," says the professor. He looks as if he's actually looking forward to this.

The End

You, Laura, and Carla scramble through the surf and crawl up on the beach.

"I know this place!" Carla shouts over the wind. "Follow me!"

You and Laura struggle to your feet and follow Carla up the beach and into a grove of palm trees, many of which have blown down. A small, conical hut built of blocks of coral cemented together is there. It looks more like an igloo at the North Pole than something you'd find in the tropics.

You all go inside through a low entranceway that faces away from the storm. Inside it is miraculously dry and warm. It has a floor of soft sand. You are all exhausted, and soon you fall into a deep sleep.

Turn to page 98.

Suddenly everything around you begins to fade. You realize to your horror that the pirates and the galleon—like the Sioux Indians in the pyramid—must, as you suspected, all be an illusion or the result of some kind of time warp. The galleon is vanishing back into time, but you are still in the present—somewhere out over the sea in the middle of a hurricane!

For a moment you hang suspended in space, looking down at the waves boiling below you—then you drop straight down into them.

You try to stay afloat, but you don't last long in the raging sea.

The End

ABOUT THE AUTHOR

RICHARD BRIGHTFIELD is a graduate of Johns Hopkins University, where he studied biology, psychology, and archaeology. For many years he worked as a graphic designer at Columbia University. He has written *The Deadly Shadow, Secret of the Pyramids, The Phantom Submarine, The Dragons' Den, The Secret Treasure of Tibet, Invaders of the Planet Earth,* and *Planet of the Dragons* in the Choose Your Own Adventure series and has coauthored more than a dozen game books with his wife, Glory. The Brightfields and their daughter, Savitri, live in Gardiner, New York.

ABOUT THE ILLUSTRATOR

LESLIE MORRILL is a designer and illustrator whose work has won him numerous awards. He has illustrated over thirty books for children, including the Bantam Classic edition of *The Wind in the Willows.* Mr. Morrill has illustrated many books in the Skylark Choose Your Own Adventure series, and *Mountain Survival, Invaders of the Planet Earth, The Brilliant Dr. Wogan, Mystery of the Sacred Stones, The Perfect Planet,* and *The First Olympics* in the Choose Your Own Adventure series. Mr. Morrill also illustrated both Super Adventure books *Journey to the Year 3000* and *Danger Zones.*

CHOOSE YOUR OWN ADVENTURE®

BANTAM
SHOP-AT-HOME
C·A·T·A·L·O·G

Shop at home
for quality children's books
and save money, too.

Now you can order books for the whole family from
Bantam's latest catalog of hundreds of titles including
many fine children's books. *And* this special offer gives
you an opportunity to purchase a Bantam book for
only 50¢. Here's how:

By ordering any five books at the regular price per
order, you can also choose any other single book listed
(up to a $5.95 value) for just 50¢. Some restrictions do
apply, so for further details send for Bantam's catalog
of titles today.